A Note from the Author

I was driving to Dorset in the summer when I got stuck in a traffic jam. There was a white van by the side of the road. The driver – a man – was standing beside the van. He was talking to a teenage girl.

On that slow, hot and boring journey, my mind began to come up with questions. Who was he? Who was she? What were they doing? What were they talking about? By the time I reached Dorset I had some story ideas. And every evening at bed time, I jotted down parts of the story in a notebook.

By the end of the week the idea was complete. I knew who the man was. I knew who the girl was. And I had my story laid out. All I had to do was to go back home and start writing it properly ...

To Sharon Smeeton

Visit Judy's website at:
www.judywaite.com

Twisting the Truth

by

Judy Waite

First published in 2010 in Great Britain by
Barrington Stoke Ltd
18 Walker Street, Edinburgh, EH3 7LP

www.barringtonstoke.co.uk

Copyright © 2010 Judy Waite

The moral right of the author has been asserted in
accordance with the Copyright, Designs and
Patents Act 1988

ISBN: 978-1-84299-760-4

Printed in Great Britain by Bell & Bain Ltd

Contents

Chapter 1
Skate Hate

"Amy Drew – I hate you," Elsa said in a whisper, even though there was no one standing near enough to hear.

She watched Amy speeding past the other skate-boarders. Elsa knew it was stupid to get so jealous. And anyway, it wasn't really true about her hating Amy. She hardly knew her. What she hated was that Amy was brilliant at skate-boarding. She looked cool and sexy. And Pete Macklin was drooling all over her.

"Come on, Pete, keep up." Amy waved a hand at Pete and did a nose-wheelie, skating forward with the tail of her board in the air. Her beautiful blonde hair was clipped back. Elsa could see her gold hooped earrings. Elsa touched her own hair. Short and brown and spiky. Why had she had it cut like that? Was someone like Pete likely to be into the "hedgehog" look?

Amy skated along the edge of the bank, then jumped and spun round. It was as if her feet were glued to the board. Pete managed the bank, but wobbled on the spin. Amy held her hand out to stop him from falling. They both laughed.

Elsa felt her tummy tie itself in knots. It really sucked, seeing the two of them get on so well. Elsa realised she was hugging her own board; the wheels pressed into her gut.

"Hey, come on, why are you just standing watching?"

Elsa felt a hand on her arm and turned to see Greg Morgan. He grinned at her. "The light will be gone soon. Let's go round together," he said.

Elsa gave a shrug. Greg was always hanging round, wanting to do stuff with her. It annoyed her that he had his hand on her arm. She moved away. "I've already been round twice," she said. "And I shouldn't really be here at all. I'm supposed to be home before dark."

"Phone your mum, then. She'll be OK when she knows there are loads of us out here. And it's Saturday. It's not like you've got school tomorrow."

"My mobile's dead. And anyway, my mum's got this new boyfriend. Steve Harley. He's round our house nearly all the time, and he's a complete control freak. Mum's at work, so he's got this idea that he's in charge of me. He'll totally flip if I'm late home."

Elsa couldn't miss the look of disappointment on Greg's face. He dropped his hand down to his side. She felt sorry. Life wasn't fair. She fancied Pete. Greg fancied her.

It would be so much easier if you just fancied the person who fancied you.

She glanced back at Amy again. Who did Amy fancy? Maybe it wasn't Pete?

But it seemed the "unfair fairy" had been waving her magic wand around making trouble for Elsa again. Amy and Pete had stopped skating and Amy was leaning against him. She laughed up at something he said. He smiled down at her. They looked like two slushy lovers in some yucky black and white film. The sort of thing Mum watched and got sniffy about on a Sunday afternoon. Or at least, she had done until she got hooked up with Steve. Since Mum had met Steve, she never sat and relaxed or enjoyed anything. She was always busy making sure the house was tidy. Making sure she had his favourite food in the house. Making sure her hair was the style Steve liked.

Elsa shivered. Thinking about Steve was almost worse than thinking about Amy and Pete. His film-star looks and dazzling blue eyes might make Mum go all silly, but Elsa didn't trust him. His good looks just seemed like a mask. A way he could trick lonely women like her mum. She turned back to Greg. "I've changed my mind. I'm going round one last time. I can hold out from going home just a tiny bit longer."

Elsa walked to the starting ramp at the other end of the track. She didn't look back to see if Greg was following, but she knew that he was. She felt cross again. Greg reminded her of a cute but annoying puppy.

He was rubbish at skate-boarding, too. Not really cool to be seen with. The only thing he was good at was cross-country running. He was in the county team, but who gave a stuff about that?

Elsa kicked forward, the rumble of her board drowning out the annoying thoughts. She wasn't a rising star at skate-boarding. She wasn't in Amy's league. But she was OK. She was as good as Pete. If he did manage to drag his slushy lover's eyes away from Amy and see Elsa spinning past, she was sure she wouldn't make a fool of herself. To be honest, though, everyone from this end of town was OK at skate-boarding. There wasn't much else to do after school, unless you were one of the wimps who were into ballet or some other equally boring thing.

Elsa pushed faster. It was chilly, and the cold stung her cheeks. She could feel the icy air catch in her throat. She liked the feeling. It was as if the air was cleaning her. Freezing out her mean thoughts and grumpy ways. She laughed out loud, skating faster and faster. Trying out all her favourite moves. She'd been stupid to get all churned up about Pete and Amy. She'd been stupid to be cross with Greg. She'd even been stupid to worry about what Steve would say if she was late. None of it mattered. Just the tricks and spins and wheelies as she whizzed round the track.

As she reached the bend where Pete and Amy were still talking, she barely looked at them. Let them snog each other's brains out. She didn't care.

And then something happened.

It came from behind, ramming into her, sending her flying face-forward. Her skate-board slipped away from her, spinning into the air. She felt herself twisting as she thumped against the bank.

"Oh, no, Elsa – are you alright? I'm so sorry."

Elsa wriggled to get out from under Greg's lumpy frame. Greg wriggled too, stood up, and held a hand out to help her to her feet. But Elsa wouldn't let him help her.

"I was just trying a new jump – a karate kick – someone at school was describing how you did it." Greg's voice was worried.

Other boarders rattled past them. A couple shouted out to see if they were OK, but no one stopped. Elsa was grateful. She hated having a fuss made of her. And she hated anyone seeing her do anything wrong. She frowned at Greg. "Well, whoever told you about it didn't do a very good job," she snapped. "You just karate-kicked me in the back."

She glanced sideways, suddenly remembering that they were right next to Pete and Amy. They must be wetting themselves laughing.

But when she looked, Elsa couldn't make up her mind which was worse. The fact that Greg had crashed into her when they were just metres away from the slushy lovers – or the fact that the slushy lovers weren't even looking at them. They were so caught up with each other, they hadn't noticed a thing.

"Oooops," Greg whispered into Elsa's ear. "Looks like we might be interrupting a private party."

Elsa stormed away from him and went to pick up her skate-board. She was wrong to have thought that Pete and Amy didn't matter. Being this close to the slushy lovers was making her hands shake and her throat go dry. It was as if her heart was being wrung out, the way Mum wrung out her school jumpers before she hung them on the line to dry.

This was what heart-ache felt like.

This was being love-sick.

And it stank.

"I'm going home." Elsa couldn't look at Greg. She was too scared that all her feelings would show in her eyes.

9

"I'll walk you back. I'm so sorry. I'm just a clumsy idiot." Greg went to touch her arm again.

Elsa pushed him away. "No. Honestly. Doesn't matter." And before he had time to do or say anything else, she ran up the bank with her board under her arm. She darted out through the skate-park entrance and into Wood Lane.

Amy Drew. I hate you. Amy Drew. I hate you. Elsa brushed her hand across her eyes. At least Greg wasn't trying to do his puppy thing and following her. At least he wouldn't see that she was crying.

Chapter 2
Jumping at Shadows

Elsa walked quickly.

The afternoon light was fading fast. The trees along the lane grew shadowy and grey. As Elsa hurried along, she wished street lamps had been put in when they'd built the skate-park. They were supposed to have been. There had been a lot of fuss about it in the local paper. But the money had run out and the skate-park had never been properly finished – not that that had ever stopped anyone from using it.

Her feet scrunched on layers of dead, frosted leaves. She suddenly wanted to tiptoe. Being out late didn't feel so good. Thinking back, perhaps staying indoors and learning something wimpy like ballet would have been a better idea after all.

And then, suddenly, her heart twisted. This wasn't the sort of slow, painful twist she had felt watching Pete with Amy. This was more of a jolt. A moment of panic.

There was somebody up ahead. Somebody watching her.

They were standing behind the fence at the edge of Mr Barker's field. What if it was a mad murderer or something?

Elsa slowed down.

Part of her wanted to turn back, but that would force her to see Pete and Amy again. And it was nearly dark. Steve would already be furious. Sometimes Elsa thought Steve was secretly always angry with her. She got in the way between him and Mum. He'd probably prefer it if she weren't there at all.

Elsa couldn't risk wasting any more time. She'd just have to cross the lane and walk on the other side.

It was probably just someone waiting for a mate to come back from the skate-park. Maybe even someone she knew from school. Nothing at all to get spooked about.

But her heart was still hammering. There was still a chance it was a murderer. She wondered if she could knock him out with her skate-board when he made a leap at her?

Would he smash her skate-board, or would he smash her skull? She gripped her board tightly, ready to start bashing if she had to.

She walked across the lane and refused to look sideways until she was almost past. And then she was so relieved, she laughed out loud.

It wasn't any creepy mad murderer. It wasn't even anyone from school. It was Mr Barker's donkey.

"You great wimp, Elsa," she muttered to herself. Turning to the donkey, she yelled, "Heehaw!" Then, just for the silliness of it, she shouted, "Heehaw!" again.

It was quite funny really, even though she was suffering from a broken heart. It was also good to know that people with broken hearts could still see the funny side of things.

She broke into a slow jog. It might only have been a donkey that had spooked her, but there was still Steve the control freak to face up to.

Elsa was still jogging when she reached the main road. Westlands Avenue. At least there were street lights there. She was getting a stitch in her side. Even though she knew she should really be sprinting home, she had to give herself a minute to catch her breath.

"Excuse me, luv ..."

The man's voice startled her.

She hadn't seen him walk towards her out of the shadows.

She wondered whether she should dodge round him, but he was right in front of her. He could easily grab her. It might be more sensible to stay calm. If he tried any funny business this was a fairly busy road. Hopefully another car would come and she could scream and wave it down.

"Excuse me ... I'm so sorry to trouble you, but I'm hoping you can help me."

They were under a street lamp and Elsa got a good look at his face. If she survived any sudden attack she might need to give details to the police. But, if she was honest, he didn't look all that scary. He was quite old, with silvery-white hair and friendly eyes.

"I'm parked over there. That's my white van in the lay-by."

Elsa stared at the van. She didn't trust this old bloke. He might be trying to trick her. The real murderer might be waiting in the van. She tried to get a look at the number-plate but it was hard to do without making it too obvious. She didn't want the old man to guess that she didn't trust him.

He waved something in the air. "I don't come from round here and my van has run out of petrol. I've got this can to fill up, but I've no idea which direction to walk in. Could you point me to the nearest petrol station?"

Elsa blinked at him. First a donkey – now a harmless old bloke who'd run out of petrol. Her imagination would have her English teacher frothing with joy. If she could only write all this down she'd be getting an A* for her next school essay.

"That way – back along this road then turn left. It's a big new Tesco. You can't miss it."

"You are an angel sent to save me." The man beamed her a warm, friendly smile. He gave a thumbs-up sign, then went.

Elsa walked on past the van, turning just once to get a look at the number-plate. She didn't even know why she did it – it just seemed mad not to, now it was so easy.

G472 PJM.

PJM – they were Pete's initials. She knew that because she and Jenni Allen had once sneaked a look at an upper school register.

PJM. Peter James Macklin.

If it hadn't been for that, she probably wouldn't have remembered it. She wasn't that great at remembering things.

But she wished it hadn't been those three letters. PJM.

They snagged at her heart. She found herself dreaming about Peter James Macklin all the way home. If only there were some way she could get Amy off the scene.

Chapter 3
White Lies

For once, the "unfair fairy" wasn't making trouble.

Steve hadn't arrived yet.

Elsa flicked the hall light on and stashed her skate-board neatly into the cupboard under the stairs. Then she pulled her trainers off and put them beside the tidy row of shoes. It didn't matter that it was just a cluttered old space where they'd used to store their junk. Steve would fly into a rage if even one wellington boot was out of order.

Hooking her jacket on the back of the kitchen door, she plugged in her mobile to re-charge the battery. Then she hurried upstairs to her room and turned on her computer.

Minutes later she was Googling "History: World War Two". Steve was a World War Two nut. He was always on about soldiers and discipline. He liked ranting about how all the losers she hung around with could do with a good battle to sort them out.

With the site safely up on her screen, she clicked on "Messenger".

Good. Jenni was on-line. Elsa could chat to Jenni about Pete and Amy. She'd pour her heart and soul out through the keyboard.

Hi Jen. u ok?

good – how r u?

gutted. Pete luvs sum 1 else. ☹

wot! how cud he?

its amy drew. frm yr 10.

sux. but thers ova fish in the c (srt of crap thng my mum says)

mine 2. y do they fink we wnt 2 go out wiv fish?

lol. ☺

At that moment Elsa heard a car door click shut. Steve had arrived. She'd forgotten how quiet his posh Toyota's engine was – not like Mum's car. She could hear that banging along from streets away.

soz. got 2 go. Mr Grumpy has cum bck. See ya X ☹

see ya X: ☹

Elsa clicked out of "Messenger" and began scrolling through "History: World War Two" as if gazing at fuzzy pictures of men in tanks was a reason for living.

"Elsa!" Steve yelled up the stairs. His voice sounded thick with fury. Ready for battle. "Come down here this minute!"

Blow it! Elsa's brilliant Google plan had back-fired. He wasn't even going to come in her room to see what a good girl she was being. But the tone of his voice was one she wouldn't risk ignoring.

She reached the top of the stairs. He scowled up at her. She'd never seen him look so angry. White-faced. His eyes were dark and strange. "Where have you been?"

"I had some problems." Elsa needed an excuse, and she struggled to think of one.

Steve still kept shouting. "I've been out looking for you. Worried sick. Driving round and round in the dark."

Elsa walked towards him down the stairs. She didn't want to get near him, but she knew he'd kick off again if she didn't. Maybe she

should tell him she fell off her skate-board?
"I'm sorry, I had a bad time. I ..."

"Don't bother. I can guess what your shoddy excuse will be. You fell off your skate-board. Or some of that sort of rubbish you tell your mother. But she's not here at the moment, and you've got me to answer to." He reached out and grabbed Elsa's arm, gripping her tightly.

"Please – let go of me." She was shaking. He'd never touched her before. He was holding her so hard, she was sure she'd bruise.

"This story you're about to come up with – it had better be good," he growled. "I tried your phone – you had it switched off. I've been driving along every street in this sodding town. I've even been stopping and asking people."

Elsa's memory was suddenly triggered. It gave her an idea. She remembered the white van man – the way he'd stopped her.

She met Steve's angry look. "If you let go of me for a second, I'll tell you what happened. The truth. It was terrible."

Steve raised his eyebrows. Elsa could see he already didn't believe her. She was going to have to work hard to get through this.

"I was walking home from the skate-park. I would have been on time, but this old bloke called out to me. He was standing beside a white van."

"Go on. And make it good."

Elsa bit her lip. She managed to get a slight tremble into her voice. And it wasn't hard to get the tears to spring into her eyes either – not with the way her arm was throbbing. "I know it was stupid, but I didn't hear what he said at first. So I went a bit nearer. He kept saying he was lost. He wanted me to look at his map. It was in the front seat of his van. I tried to tell him I didn't want to get in beside him, but he was gripping my arm." She looked down at where Steve was gripping her.

He looked too. She felt him relax his hold.

"What happened next?" Steve's voice seemed shaky and strange.

"I – I kicked him. I think he was shocked. He swore at me, but I managed to break away. And I ran."

"Am I hearing this right? Some pervert tried to force you into his van?"

Elsa nodded. It wasn't hard to lie. Not really. After all, she'd already partly imagined it happening. "I ran for about five minutes, but then I got a stitch. I couldn't breathe. So I dived down between the newsagent and the hairdresser's. You know – that alley there? I hid in there. I didn't know what else to do."

"Did he go looking for you? Did you see him drive past?" Steve had let go of her completely now. He was staring at her.

"No. I hid there for ages. I was so scared. In the end I got so cold I just took a risk and came the long way home."

"And this pervert – where exactly did he stop you?"

"He was parked in the lay-by along Westlands Avenue. Just past the entrance to Wood Lane."

Steve pulled his car keys from his pocket, and turned towards the front door. Then he stopped again, turning back, "I don't suppose you looked at the number plate?"

"Most of it. G something something something PJM. I've forgotten the numbers bit."

Steve nodded. "Good girl. Now stay here, in the house."

"Where are you going?"

"To find him, of course. See what he thinks he was playing at." He hesitated, then added, "Best you don't ring your mum or anything, though. Don't want her worrying. You know what she's like."

Elsa stared after him as the front door closed. Steve's Toyota purred softly into life. How typical of Steve to want to get the bloke himself, rather than ringing the police. At least that was a good thing. She'd been quite proud of herself telling the story, but the last thing she'd want to do was repeat it to the police.

Elsa had one terrible, heart-chilling thought where she imagined Steve catching up with the old bloke and giving him a going-over. She tried not to think about his friendly smile. She tried not to think about how he'd look with all his teeth knocked out. But it wouldn't happen. The man would have gone to Tesco, got back and filled his tank by now. He'd be headed on to wherever it was he was going.

He wasn't local, so there was no chance Steve would see him driving round the town.

Was there?

Chapter 4
Bad News

Steve didn't do over the old van driver.

He came back with fish and chips instead.

Elsa hurried to lay the table.

Steve stopped her. "Let's have this on our laps and watch TV together," he said.

Elsa stared at him. Had he just had a personality transplant or something? Maybe aliens had beamed up the other Steve and sent this fake one in his place? Who cared? She was getting fish and chips. She was going to pig out in front of the box. And for the first time since Mum had hooked up with Steve, she considered the idea that perhaps he wasn't such a nightmare after all.

They watched a quiz show and a science thing to do with cars of the future. They were both a bit boring but Elsa didn't complain. At least she wasn't being force-fed World War Two documentaries.

"I'll clear these dishes." Steve got up from his chair. "I want to make sure it's all put away before your mum gets back."

Elsa stared at him again. If this went any further he'd be suggesting they all play Scrabble later.

She decided it was best not to encourage him too much. There were limits, after all. "If it's OK with you, I'll go back on my computer."

She waited for the fuss about how computers were bad for her brain. She waited for the warning about "dodgy sites". She waited for the threat that he knew how to check up on what she'd been Googling.

Instead he just smiled – which was a bit scary. "Don't stay on it for too long. You don't want to strain your eyes."

Elsa scampered up the stairs. It was best that she got out of his way as quickly as possible. She didn't want to risk doing anything that might make his mood swing back again.

She clicked on "Messenger".

Hi Jen. r u thr?

Jenni didn't answer. Elsa thought about texting her and telling her to go online, and then remembered her phone was charging downstairs. It was safer to stay where she was.

She Googled skate-boarding sites instead. They had some really cool boards for sale. Hers had been second-hand from a car boot sale, but if Steve was going to stay in alien brain mode, maybe she could ask for an expensive one for Christmas. Steve liked expensive things.

It wasn't just his super-smooth Toyota. Mum was always going on about his posh flat on the other side of town. He even insisted on buying new clothes for Mum, complaining her old stuff was tacky.

So maybe he'd feel the same about Elsa's tatty old skate-board? And even if he didn't, it was nice to hope.

She kept Googling. Pictures of cool, sexy boards filled her screen.

Elsa was so lost in the dream about owning a top-of-the-range Blue Devil that she didn't realise Mum was standing in the doorway until she called her name. "Elsa!"

"Hi, how was work?" Elsa half-raised one hand, without turning round.

"Elsa – there's someone here for you. Downstairs."

"For me?"

"It's the police."

Elsa spun round and stared at Mum. "Why – what's happened?"

"It's about a girl from your school. Apparently you left the skate-park just before she did."

"So?"

"She hasn't arrived home."

Elsa shivered, as if an icy finger had run down her spine. She remembered how spooky Wood Lane had felt. Maybe her instincts had picked up on something bad after all?

"Who is the girl?"

Mum shook her head. "Not anyone I'd heard of. I think she's a bit older than you. Her name is Amy Drew."

A policewoman greeted Elsa in the front room. "I'm PC Duncan. This is my colleague, PC Jones."

Elsa looked at the other officer. He gave her a friendly smile, but she couldn't return it. She was feeling too sick. Her mind was filled with shadowy pictures of what Amy might be going through. She'd been so wrong to have those bad thoughts about her. What if something really horrible had happened?

And on top of that – Elsa was about to get into mega-trouble. She was going to have to admit that she'd lied about the white van man.

Steve appeared with cups of tea for the officers. He seemed wound-up.

Elsa guessed it was because he was near people in uniform. The police must be as exciting to him as soldiers were. She guessed too that "alien brain nice Steve" had probably been taken over by the control freak once again. And if he wasn't yet, he soon would be, once she admitted the truth. The sick feeling rolled over her. Her hands shook.

"Sit down, Elsa, there's nothing to worry about." PC Duncan nodded at PC Jones, who switched on a small black recorder. "We need to tape this interview, so we can go over it again later. Are you happy with that?"

Elsa nodded. Her mouth was dry with fear. Was lying about why you were late home a criminal offence?

She sat on the edge of the sofa.

She felt everyone watching her, waiting for what she was going to say.

PC Duncan checked her name and her age.

She asked about the skate-park. Who had been there? What time had Elsa left? Where had she gone?

Elsa answered quietly, and stared down at the carpet.

She could hear Steve breathing.

Would he start shouting with the police still there?

"Our information is that there was a young man talking to Amy at the track. Peter Macklin. Did you notice if the two of them were fighting, or looked unhappy together?"

Elsa looked up suddenly. Did the police think Pete was involved? "Pete's great," she said quickly. However hacked off she'd been about him and Amy, there was no way they were going to get her to bad-mouth him. "He'd never hurt anyone."

PC Duncan met her gaze. Elsa saw that she raised her eyebrows slightly. Then she got back to the questions. "And once you were walking home, Elsa – did you see anything odd?"

Elsa was silent for a moment.

She saw Steve looking at her. His eyes were glittery bright. "It's all right, Elsa. I've told them."

Elsa swallowed. How was she going to un-tell his story to PC Duncan? "I ... it wasn't ..." She trailed off miserably, staring at the carpet again.

"You don't need to worry about anything. Mr Harley has given us a lot of information. Even the van number plate. You're a very clever girl to remember detail like that. All I need now is for you to tell me exactly what happened."

Elsa closed her eyes. She could picture the old man really clearly. She remembered his friendly eyes. It wouldn't take them long to trace him. She imagined the police car screaming up behind him on the motorway. Or maybe it would be an officer hammering on the door of his house?

Elsa knew her voice was shaking. "I didn't really ..."

Suddenly PC Duncan's police radio bleeped. "Excuse me, Elsa – I must just take this. It might be important."

Elsa sat, cloaked in misery, listening to the one-sided conversation. "I see. Yes. Excellent. Better than we could have hoped for."

She turned to Elsa again. "Important news," she said, looking grim. "Just before you came down, I phoned through the information Mr Harley gave us. An officer went to the lay-by in question. He has just found a gold hooped earring in the gutter. There were other items at the scene too that we know belong to Amy Drew. Forensics have been called, and will be checking them through.

They check everything – they know how to look for clues." She gave a small, tight smile. "I know it's distressing news, but it's perfect evidence for us. This man is the one we want. And because of you, we're going to find him easily."

Elsa blinked up at PC Duncan.

She heard Steve give a long, low breath. Like a sigh of relief. This mattered more to him that she'd realised. He really was a nicer person than she'd thought.

And the white van man? Well, she'd been wrong about him too.

The evidence was clear.

He might be doing something terrible to Amy that very second. What if he was raping her? What if he was killing her? The cold-spine-finger feeling grew worse. Elsa started shaking all over. He must have wanted to do those things to her too. So it didn't matter now if she stuck to her lie. White van man was wicked and evil. Elsa had the power to make sure he was stopped.

"It was terrible," she began, looking steadily at PC Duncan. "He tried to trick me. I thought I was going to die."

Chapter 5
School Crowd

It was Monday morning.

"Are you sure you're OK?" Mum stopped the car as near to the school gates as she could get.

There was a white van parked across the street. It wasn't the same size as the one the old man had been driving. It wasn't the same type.

But Elsa still shivered when she saw it. Last night she had had a dream that the old man came looking for her. He was smiling. He had blood on his lips.

"I'm fine, Mum. Thanks for the lift." Elsa got out of the car and hurried past the van without looking in.

Jenni and Greg were standing just inside the gates, waiting for her. There was a huddle of other pupils standing with them. Most of them were the other skate-boarders from Saturday afternoon.

They crowded round, firing questions. Bobby Hill sounded impressed. "You mean you saw him?"

Elsa looked back just as a boy from the first year climbed out of the white van and waved at the driver. It was just someone's dad. Nothing to worry about. But she shivered again.

The huddle kept pace with her as she walked towards the school building.

"Do you think he's attacked Amy?" Lucy Crabb asked.

"I bet he's raped her," Kelly Foster added.

Bobby sounded even more impressed. "Do you think she'll have been stabbed, or strangled?"

Elsa got a picture in her mind. It was the old man, grinning at her. It was a scary grin. He was lifting his arms, but this time it wasn't to wave a petrol can at her. It was to reach forward and tighten his hands around her neck.

She tried to walk faster, to get away from all the questions, but everyone else just walked faster too. They kept up their flow of questions and comments. Kelly frowned. "Did the old guy seem violent?"

"I bet she's dead by now," Lucy sighed.

"Elsa, you could be dead by now too." Greg was the only one who sounded worried.

"I should have walked you home. I should have looked after you."

"If you'd done that, she'd never have got the van's number-plate," Kelly argued. "The police wouldn't have any leads."

"Every girl in this school would be in danger," Bobby butted in.

"We still are," said Jenni, as they reached the main doors. "The old pervert hasn't been found yet. He might have had a false number-plate or something."

Lucy gazed at Elsa as if she was a super-hero. "But you were amazing for remembering that number."

Jenni touched Elsa's arm. "Come on. Let's go somewhere quieter. You'll be signing autographs in a minute."

Elsa let Jenni lead her away. She couldn't think straight. She kept thinking about Amy being strangled and left in a ditch. Or lying in a pool of blood with a knife in her chest. What if that number-plate *was* false? White van man could be waiting for her around any corner. Would she be next on his list?

They walked down the corridor towards the girls' loo.

"Elsa?" The voice came from behind her. Elsa looked round – and her heart did a double somersault.

Pete was standing there. "Can we talk?"

All the horror film thoughts drained away. Elsa felt Jenni poke her in the ribs. She didn't dare look at her because she was scared she'd suddenly giggle. She ran her fingers backwards through her hedgehog hair, then realised she'd probably just made it stick up more than ever. And then she remembered Amy, and she felt ashamed for thinking about something so pathetic as her hair.

"I'll go on ahead." Jenni poked her again. "Text me when you're ready."

Jenni swung away, leaving Elsa and Pete staring at each other.

Elsa's knees felt like jelly. She was sure she must be blushing like a beetroot.

The skate-board crowd spotted them. Bobby shouted, "Hey, Pete. We heard you'd been locked up. Tell us all about it." Everyone hurried down the corridor towards them.

"How come the police let you go?" Lucy was the first to reach them.

"Have you heard anything about Amy?" Kelly elbowed her out of the way.

Pete sounded tired. "I was taken in for questioning. They released me yesterday morning. I don't know anything else. Now give me some space. I'm shattered."

A few of the skate-board crowd shook Pete's hand or patted him on the back. Then they all shuffled off, muttering.

"Come on. Let's go somewhere private." Pete steered Elsa back out of the main doors, and out towards the playing fields.

It felt brilliant to have him brush against her as they walked.

It was cold, the grass crunchy with morning frost.

"Let's sit here." Pete pointed to a bench near the staff car park.

Elsa sat down next to him. She felt stupidly shy. She hoped he wasn't going to expect her to say anything intelligent. Having him this close had turned her brain into a wobbling blob.

Pete turned to her. "I wanted to thank you."

"For what?" Elsa stared back at him, noticing for the first time how pale he looked. How hollow his eyes were. And how sad.

He reached across and squeezed her fingers. Elsa blinked down at his hand holding hers. It was a warm feeling. If only it had been for a different reason. "They tried to pin it on me at first," he said softly. "I was the prime suspect."

"Why?" Elsa frowned

"I was the last person Amy was seen with. I left with her. I did walk her nearly as far as Westlands Avenue. I was running late, though. I was supposed to be at a family party, so I said goodbye to her just past old Barker's field. I would never have let her go all the way along Wood Lane on her own, but I couldn't imagine anything happening to her out on that main road." He thumped his knee with his fist, as if he was trying to beat himself up.

Elsa felt a pain in her heart, just hearing the hurt in his voice. The pain was partly for him – and partly for her. But she knew too that it suddenly wasn't important that he didn't fancy her. He was special. She was lucky to know him. And maybe, once all the nightmare stuff had settled, they could at least be mates.

"Hey – you two!"

Elsa looked up and saw Greg hurrying towards them.

As he reached them, Elsa saw him glance down at where Pete was still holding her hand. She saw how his face turned pale before he looked away. And she heard the hurt in his voice when he spoke. "Miss Lewis sent me out to get you. The police are on their way. There's been some news."

Chapter 6
The Face to Fear

Elsa sat in the back of the police car. PC Duncan was the driver. PC Jones sat next to her. PC Duncan started the engine, and they drove away through the school gates.

"I don't get it," said Elsa to PC Jones. "You said Amy was found in Barker's field. You said she was lying in the donkey shed. Knocked out. But surely the sniffer dogs would have found her in there on Saturday night?"

PC Jones looked round at Elsa. "She hasn't been there all the time. We think she was dumped early this morning. She's been kept somewhere else. She's come round a bit since she's been in hospital, but she's still very confused."

"At least she's alive." Elsa remembered all the talk about stabbing and strangling from earlier on. She thought about how Pete must be feeling. She was happy for him. Really happy. Although she still wouldn't wash the hand he'd been holding for at least a week.

"Amy is very lucky." PC Duncan interrupted Elsa's new daydream. "For some reason her attacker let her go."

"Why would he do that?" Elsa thought the easiest thing would surely be to kill someone once you'd kidnapped them? How else could you make sure they wouldn't talk?

"He gave her a lot of drugs to knock her out. It's possible he saw Amy as an experiment. He may have really wanted to get someone else. No doubt we'll find out more as the investigation goes on." PC Duncan turned the car siren on, and they sped down the streets, jumping a red traffic light. "After you've helped in the identity parade this morning, we'll be able to follow a more direct line of questioning with our main suspect."

Elsa didn't answer. Her throat went dry. She was relieved they'd managed to catch white van man that morning too, but she wasn't looking forward to getting face-to-face with him. Not even from the safety of a police station.

They sped on through the town. PC Duncan kept the siren on. Elsa could see people staring at them, trying to guess what was going on. Normally it would have been exciting, but today it just meant they'd get to the police station sooner. Elsa would be in the same building as white van man. Just because he hadn't killed Amy, it didn't mean he hadn't done something bad. He'd hardly snatched her so he could take her home for tea and cake.

And according to PC Duncan, they didn't have enough evidence to arrest him yet. There was a problem with matching the fingerprints. There was a problem with the inside of the van. It was only Elsa's evidence that could really nail him. And if the police couldn't make the charge stick, he'd be free to go. Free to come looking for Elsa. Free to make her sorry for getting him caught …

She saw his face in her mind again. This time he had pointed teeth. Fanged teeth. And they dripped blood all through her imagination.

Minutes later, they were pulling into the police station car park.

"There's nothing to worry about." PC Jones came round and opened Elsa's door. "It will soon all be over."

They went into the building. PC Jones said something to the officer behind the front desk, then PC Duncan led Elsa up some stairs. They went into a narrow room with one long window. "Everything's in place." PC Duncan handed Elsa a pad and paper. "You don't even need to speak. All you have to do is look through that window at the men in the line-up. Each one will be holding a number. If you recognise the man from Saturday night, just write his number on the pad. Is that clear?"

Elsa's gut was knotting up. She trembled. Her heart seemed to be missing beats. "I'm scared he'll see me."

"No chance. This window is one-way. You can see out, but no one can see in. You're completely safe."

Elsa battled her fear. She had to do this. If she didn't, she'd never be free of the blood and fang nightmares.

There were six men. They stood in a straight line, staring blankly in front of them. They were all old. The same sort of height. The same white hair. But it didn't matter that there were six similar oldies in the identity line-up. Only one of them was important. And Elsa knew exactly which one he was.

She thought she'd just scrawl down the number and back away from the window, but to her surprise she found herself examining him. She'd expected to see a monster. She'd expected to see some sort of evil glow round him. A cruel twist to his lips, or a steel glint in his eye. She couldn't pick out any of that. He just looked scared. Small and frail and worried. But then she told herself that was the trick he played. He was an actor. A fraud. In a way, that was scarier than a fanged monster. You'd never stop to help a fanged monster find its way somewhere.

With that thought in her head, Elsa wrote the number 4 on the pad. She stepped back from the window.

PC Duncan took the pad. "You've been an excellent witness," she smiled. "Your evidence will make all the difference. I'm going to settle you in the interview room. Mr Harley is driving over to pick you up."

Elsa followed PC Duncan back down the stairs and into another room. Steve had been great since Saturday night. And he'd been so worried about Amy, too. He'd been up before dawn, ready to join the first search-party of the day.

PC Duncan stood by the door. "Sit yourself down. There are some magazines on the table. I have to fill in some reports now, but I'll be in touch soon."

"Thanks." Once PC Duncan had gone, Elsa tried to read the magazine, but she couldn't focus.

She couldn't even look at the pictures. All she could see was the old man's face with his worried eyes. It still bothered her that he didn't look like a pervert.

But then, the more she thought about it, she realised she didn't know what any sort of criminal looked like. Muggers. Bank robbers. Murderers. They could all walk past her in the street and she wouldn't have a clue who they really were.

She was relieved when the door opened and Steve walked in. "Sorry to take so long – I just had some clearing-up to do at my flat. I'm going to be selling it soon."

Elsa nodded. Just a week ago she'd have been horrified that he was selling his flat. She'd have been horrified because it would have meant he planned to move in with her and Mum, and stay there forever.

Now it was OK.

Everything was OK.

"You ready?" He smiled.

"You bet." She smiled back.

She couldn't wait to get away from this scary perv-catching place, and get her life back to normal again.

Chapter 7
The Dragon's Den

Steve's Toyota purred its way along Westlands Avenue. It smelt clean. A shampoo-fresh smell. They passed the entrance to Wood Lane. It was all taped off. Elsa could see a couple of police cars parked near Barker's field.

Steve hadn't asked her loads of questions, and she was grateful for that.

She felt weird now it was all over. Different. She wasn't the same girl who'd stood jealously watching Amy and Pete together. Anything could happen to anyone, at any time. She was never going to be nasty like that again.

"Are you hungry?" Steve glanced sideways at her. "We could stop and eat somewhere?"

Elsa shook her head. She was still feeling a bit sick and shaky. "I've got sandwiches and stuff. I'll have them when I get back to school."

"You don't need to go back this morning. I could ring in for you. We could do something together," Steve said.

Elsa shook her head again. The new changed Elsa still couldn't face spending a whole day with Steve. He'd probably suggest a "fun" outing, and end up dragging her round a museum or something. "I need to get back. We've got maths and then English. I can't miss either of them."

In her head, Elsa pictured what Jenni would do if she'd heard her say that. She'd snort with laughter. She'd probably even collapse on the floor. In fact, Elsa would collapse with her. They'd get stitches in their sides, just rolling about giggling.

Thinking about it made her smile.

It might not be true about the maths and the English – but she *did* want to get back to her mates. She wanted to have a laugh with Jenni. To be where Pete was. And she was even missing Greg a bit too.

"You seem relaxed now. That's good." Steve glanced at her again. And then, to Elsa's shock, he took one hand from the steering wheel and rested it on her knee.

She felt herself freeze inside. Was Steve allowed to touch her now that he would be living with them soon? It didn't feel right. It didn't feel good. She'd felt so warm when Pete had touched her. She felt so cold now.

After a moment she shifted her leg a little, moving it away. Steve lifted his hand and put it back on the steering wheel. Elsa felt sorry for him. She was being mean again. Poor bloke was doing his best to be friendly.

"Do you mind if I get something to eat? I've been so busy in the flat all morning, I haven't even had a coffee." Steve interrupted her thoughts.

"No. Sure. That's fine." Elsa was keen to make up for feeling weird about him touching her. At least he didn't seem upset.

They turned off Westlands Avenue and drove along one of the smaller roads. Elsa was surprised. "There will be more eating places in town, won't there?"

"I know a fantastic Chinese – a bit off the beaten track, but it's worth it. Its sweet and sour chicken is to die for. Once you smell it you'll be all over me, begging me to let you share it." Steve laughed.

It was an odd sound. It struck Elsa that she'd never heard him laugh before. It felt wrong, hearing it come out of his mouth. As they flashed past trees and fields and farms, the whole journey suddenly felt wrong. Where was he taking her? What was going on?

"Here we are." Steve slowed the Toyota, and drew up outside a small row of shops.

One of them had a green dragon painted on the window. Its sign said:

Green Dragon – Chinese food to take away.

Elsa felt sorry for not trusting Steve again. This whole Amy thing had made her twitchy. She'd have to get herself sorted.

"You sure you don't want anything?" Steve switched off the engine.

"No. Honestly. I'm really not hungry."

"All right. I'll leave the car doors unlocked. That way you can come in and find me if you get lonely." He gave that same odd laugh again, got out of the Toyota, and went across to the take-away.

Elsa sat and waited. Steve was taking ages. They must have gone off to catch the chicken before they cooked it, or something.

She wondered if he had a newspaper in the back of the Toyota, and leaned over to have a look. Nothing. The back seat was spotless. She wondered if he cleaned it himself. There wasn't even the smallest speck of dirt on the floor. She leant further, twisting so she could run her fingers across the perfect carpet. Just to kill time.

Her fingers touched something that felt like metal, out of sight under the driver's seat. Ha! She'd found proof that Steve was at least human. It must be a scrap of wire, or something.

Her fingers closed round it.

It was a gold hooped earring.

Chapter 8
Running Scared

Horror rolled over Elsa.

There was only one reason why a gold hooped earring would be in the back of Steve's Toyota.

And suddenly everything made sense.

The way he'd come home, all wound up and angry on Saturday night.

The way he'd gone storming out to look for "white van man".

The other earring and extra "items" by the lay-by that he must have put there himself.

The way he'd been so keen to tell the police what she had told him.

And it was Elsa's fault. Her lie had given everything to him on a plate. A take-away dish of false evidence that Steve could use to protect himself. But why had he done it? Why had he taken Amy like that? And then she remembered PC Duncan saying that perhaps it had been an experiment. Perhaps he'd been practising. Perhaps it was Elsa he'd *really* wanted to get rid of.

Her whole body shook.

Looking over towards the Green Dragon, she could see him inside. Any second now he'd be paying for his food. Any second now he'd be walking back out.

Elsa fumbled for the door handle.

Still clutching the earring, she clambered from the Toyota and raced away down the lane.

She'd never run so fast. Not even on sports day. Running as if her life depended on it. In fact, her life probably did depend on it.

He'd be bound to guess. He'd be bound to come after her.

There were thick hedges along the edges of the fields. The lane was bumpy. A couple of times she stumbled. A car rumbled up behind her. Should she jump in a hedge? Would he see her?

The car pulled out around her. It wasn't Steve. Not this time.

It hurt to breathe. Elsa's feet hurt. For the first time ever she wished she hadn't insisted on school shoes with heels. She should kick them off – she'd be faster then – but was there time to stop?

Suddenly she saw a small muddy track in between the hedges.

She stumbled down it. This was her only chance.

Even if Steve spotted it, it would take him minutes to park the Toyota. Precious minutes that might save her. Pausing just long enough to pull off the shoes, she kept going, scanning the fields for tractors driven by friendly farmers.

There was no one – just fields and fields. In the sky she saw crows circling, like vultures. They must be able to smell her fear.

Her feet stung. Pain throbbed in her side. She felt dizzy and sick. She had to stop, or she'd collapse.

To the right of her was a small clump of trees. Elsa knew what she could do – she could dive in there and ring the police on her mobile. Why hadn't she thought of that before?

Darting sideways, she hid amongst a tangle of bushes. Then she dropped to her knees, searching in her pocket for her phone. Her hands shook so much she could barely punch the keys. She held the phone to her ear – but there was no ringing. No friendly voice on the other end.

Her phone had no signal in this stupid miles from anywhere place. There was no chance of getting help.

And she heard the sound of running footsteps.

Chapter 9
Time for Truths

Elsa shrank back into the brambles. The branches scratched her face. She clamped her hand across her mouth to try and muffle the sound of her ragged breathing.

His body was almost level with her now, moving past the gap. Her eyes were wide with horror as she waited for him to guess where she was. And then, as she saw the person properly, her eyes grew even wider. She screamed, pure shock forcing his name from her lips. "Greg!"

For a moment she thought he was going to run on by, and she scrabbled to her feet, ready to scream again.

But in seconds Greg had stopped. Turned back. Pushed in through the gap. "Elsa? What are you doing in there?" He stood, confused, taking in her scratched, messed-up face.

Elsa stumbled towards him.

He folded his arms round her.

She'd never been held by anyone so strong or so firm. It was like being hugged by a tree.

"I can't believe it." Her voice caught in short, breathless sobs. "What are *you* doing here?"

Greg stepped back slightly so he could get a better look at her, "This is one of my cross-country running tracks. I train here every week. But what's happened?"

Elsa sobbed out the story about Steve and the gold hooped earrings, and her lie about white van man.

Greg took her arm. "There's no way Steve will hurt you, not when you're with me. And I'm not on my own. My whole team will be thundering past any minute. I just happened to be in the lead. There's a place further back where mobiles can pick up a signal. We'll go there and call the police. The other guys will wait with us." Then, noticing she was limping, he stopped again, and stooped over a bit. "Come on – get on my back – I'll carry you."

Elsa held on tight, as he piggy-backed her to the world of mobile signals and normal roads and normal people.

She was still feeling sick and shaky. She was going to get into a heap of trouble about the poor white van man. And there were other horrible things she'd have to face too.

Mum would be gutted.

73

Maybe Pete and Amy would hate her.

Maybe everyone at school would hate her.

Even Jenni would be hurt that she hadn't shared the truth with her.

As they rounded a corner, Greg slowed from a jog to a walk. "Your phone will work now," he said, stopping so she could slip off his back.

He took her hand as she went to punch the numbers on her mobile. "Let me do it. You're still shaking."

She stood waiting while he made the call. He didn't let go of her hand. Not even when he'd finished speaking. Not even when the rest of his team began turning up, wanting to know what was going on.

"Thanks for – you know – not judging me," she said softly, as they all walked back to the road to wait for the police.

Greg squeezed her fingers. It was a warm feeling. "That's what mates are for," he said.

Elsa squeezed Greg's fingers back. A mate like him was more than she deserved.

She was going to make sure she treated him properly from now on.

And maybe the "unfair fairy" would give them both a break in the end.

Barrington Stoke would like to thank all its readers for commenting on the manuscript before publication and in particular:

Alianaz Alam

Jamie Anderson

Kimberly Black

Josh Clark

Sarah Cunningham

Anne-Marie Mary Dawson

Kelly Dawson

Liz Devine

Christine Douglas

Laura Grant

Ferdusi Nisa Jaham

Lesley Kettley

Alanna Laidlaw

Nida Mumtaz

Nicola Oliver

Iain Petrie

Stacy Powell

Cherie Robertson

Bobby Shaw

Martin Smith

Marcus Wishart

Become a Consultant!

Would you like to be a consultant? Ask your parent, carer or teacher to contact us at the email address below – we'd love to hear from them! They can also find out more by visiting our website.

schools@barringtonstoke.co.uk
www.barringtonstoke.co.uk

Getting Away With It
by Anne Cassidy

Mark's girlfriend is dead. And it's his fault.
He stole the car. He took his eyes off the road. He crashed.
But it was she he left in the snow before walking away. But he can't walk away from the truth. It's ripping him apart. Will she haunt him forever?

Them and Us
by Bali Rai

David's always the new boy. He and his mum keep moving to get away from his abusive dad. David thinks he can deal with anything. But this time he's the only white boy at his new school. And some people have a problem with that. Can David beat the racist bullies?

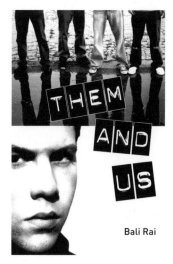

You can order these books directly from our website at
www.barringtonstoke.co.uk